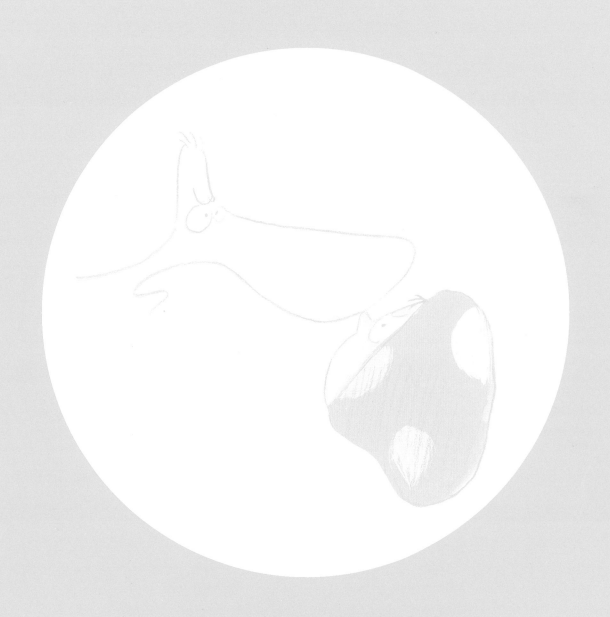

How Selfish!

For the one and only, Jimmy Welsh. – C.H.W.

Quarto is the authority on a wide range of topics.

Quarto educates, entertains and enriches the lives of our readers—enthusiasts and lovers of hands-on living.

www.quartoknows.com

First Published in 2020 by words & pictures,

an imprint of The Quarto Group.

26391 Crown Valley Parkway, Suite 220, Mission Viejo, CA 92691, USA

T: +1 949 380 7510

F: +1 949 380 7575

www.quartoknows.com

A CIP record for this book is available from the Library of Congress.

ISBN: 978 0 7112 4447 4

9 8 7 6 5 4 3 2 1

Manufactured in Guangdong, China CC022020

MIX
Paper from responsible sources
FSC
www.fsc.org
FSC® C008047

Clare Helen Welsh • Olivier Tallec

How Selfish!

words & pictures

"Hi, Dot. What shall we do today?"

"Mine!"

"Fffffffffff!"

How selfish!

"Look, a stick!"

"Let's make a flag..."

"No, that's my sword."

How selfish!

"Flag."

"Sword."

"Flag!"

"Sword!"

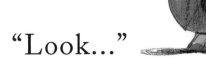

"Look..."

"SWORD!"

"Ouch! You hurt me..."

"Ha! Hi yah! Take that!
It's MY sword and you can't have it!"

How selfish!

"Swap the flag
for a rabbit?"

"That's MY toy!"

"The flag for a game?"

"Give me back MY ball!"

How selfish!

"Maybe we could share?"

"Okay! You have the leaf. I'll have EVERYTHING else."

"But I want the flag..."

"Too late. It's gone."

How selfish!

"I'm telling on you..."

"No! Wait! Don't tell!
I'll share the toys..."

"Have ALL the toys!
Have whatever you want!"

"But NOT the sword!"

"IT. IS. A. FLAG!"

"Fine. But I want ALL my things back."

"Deal?"

"Thank you, but..."

"Ha! Hi ya! Take that!"

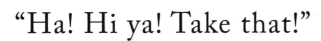

"They're MY toys and you can't have them!"

How... selfish...

How boring...

How lonely...

If only there was someone to play with...

SNAP!

"A sword! How exciting!"

"A flag! How thoughtful!"

"Dot and Duck
forever!"

How fun!

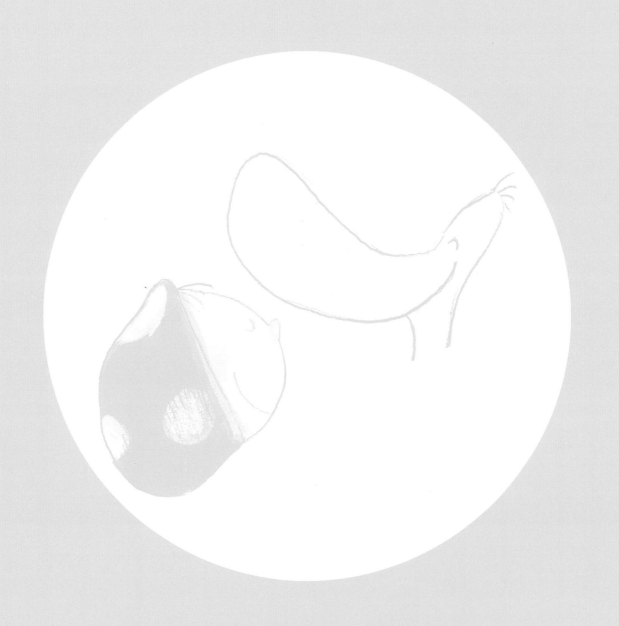